H.   was born in Dublin and grew up in southern England.
She s   and Design at the University of Sunderland, graduating
w   ours. In 2013 she gained a Master of Fine Art with
Dist   burgh College of Art, and in the same year she was
Highly   the Macmillan Illustration Prize and was a winner of
the Seven   Lincoln Illustration Competition. Holly also competes
for her co   she is a double National Champion and Gold, Silver
and Bro   at World and European Championships. She lives in
Sunderla   ook, *15 Things Not to Do with a Baby*, was selected as
on   est children's books of 2015 by *The Independent*.
H   the first book she has both written and illustrated.

For May, Max, Beth, Osca
and dog lovers everywhere! — H.S.

JANETTA OTTER-BARRY BOOKS

First published in Great Britain and in the USA in 2016 by
Frances Lincoln Children's Books
This first paperback edition published in Great Britain in 2017 by
Frances Lincoln Children's Books, 74-77 White Lion Street, London N1 9PF
QuartoKnows.com
Visit our blogs at QuartoKnows.com

A CIP catalogue record for this book is available from the British Library.

ISBN 978-1-84780-675-8

Illustrated with watercolour, pencil and 'printed' textures.

Printed in China

1 3 5 7 9 8 6 4 2

HiCcups!

Holly Sterling

Frances Lincoln
Children's Books

One morning Ruby and Oscar were playing
their favourite game, when all of a sudden...

"Oh dear, Oscar!" said Ruby.
"How are we going to get rid of those hiccups?"

"I know, why don't we try **dancey-dancing** like this?" said Ruby.

Hic!

Oscar danced just like Ruby, but the hiccups did not stop.

"How about if we jumpity-jump like this?" said Ruby.
Oscar jumped just like Ruby, but the hiccups were still there.

Hic!

"What if we **slurpity-slurp** like this?" said Ruby.

Hic!

Hic!

Hic!

Oscar slurped through his straw,
but that didn't work either.

Ruby and Oscar twirly-twirled

Hic!

and hoppity-hopped.

Hic!

They **munchy-munched**

Hic!

and **tickly-tickled**

Hic!

but NOTHING could make Oscar's hiccups disappear!

Ruby stopped to think.

"Aha!" she said.
"I know exactly what will
get rid of your hiccups."

Ruby went to her toy box in search of her...

magic wand and wizard's hat.
With a *swish* and a *swoosh* she waved her wand.

Ruby threw her wand to the ground and tried a very loud

stompity-stomp instead.

But...

Oscar just could not stop!

Hic!

Hic!

Hic!

Then Ruby had a really BRILLIANT idea.

She ran away and came back
wearing her special furry...

dress-up cat costume!

"Meeeoooow!"

she shouted.

Oscar was a bit scared!
His ears blew back and his tail
gave a very small wiggle-waggle...

but he DIDN'T hiccup!

"They've gone!" said Ruby. "Your hiccups have gone!"
And she gave Oscar a great big hug.

"Woof! Woof!" barked Oscar.

Feeling very pleased with themselves, Ruby and Oscar went back to playing their favourite game,

until all of a sudden...

"Hic!"

said Ruby.

Also illustrated by Holly Sterling for
FRANCES LINCOLN CHILDREN'S BOOKS

15 Things Not to Do with a Baby

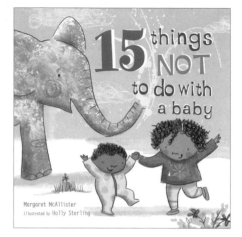

978-1-84780-753-3

CONGRATULATIONS! You now have a new
baby in your family. Just follow our simple tips
and you'll all be very happy…

DON'T send your baby to play with an elephant,
lend him to a kangaroo, or give the baby to an
octopus to cuddle. And never let your baby
take the dog for a walk!

"A humorous take on the conflicting emotions
that younger siblings can inspire."
— *Independent on Sunday*

15 Things Not to Do with a Granny

978-1-84780-852-3

A granny is a wonderful person to have in your
life. Just follow these simple rules and you'll
both be very happy…

DON'T hide an elephant in Granny's bed, give her
jelly beans for breakfast, or wear her pants
on your head. And never send her to the moon
in a rocket!

This funny, warm-hearted picture book is perfect
for the whole family to share.

Frances Lincoln titles are available from all good bookshops.
You can also buy books and find out more about your favourite titles,
authors and illustrators on our website: www.franceslincoln.com